WELCOME TO
PASSPORT TO READING
A beginning reader's ticket to a brand-new world!

Every book in this program is designed to build read-along and read-alone skills, level by level, through engaging and enriching stories. As the reader turns each page, he or she will become more confident with new vocabulary, sight words, and comprehension.

These PASSPORT TO READING levels will help you choose the perfect book for every reader.

READING TOGETHER
Read short words in simple sentence structures together to begin a reader's journey.

READING OUT LOUD
Encourage developing readers to sound out words in more complex stories with simple vocabulary.

READING INDEPENDENTLY
Newly independent readers gain confidence reading more complex sentences with higher word counts.

READY TO READ MORE
Readers prepare for chapter books with fewer illustrations and longer paragraphs.

This book features sight words from the educator-supported Dolch Sight Words List. This encourages the reader to recognize commonly used vocabulary words, increasing reading speed and fluency.

For more information, please visit www.passporttoreadingbooks.com, where each reader can add stamps to a personalized passport while traveling through story after story!

Enjoy the journey!

The First Adventures of
SPIDER

West African Folktales
Retold by

Joyce Cooper Arkhurst

Illustrated by
Caldecott Medal Winner

Jerry Pinkney

LB

LITTLE, BROWN AND COMPANY
New York · Boston

To all the friends in Liberia and Ghana who told me so many stories on so many moonlit nights.

This book is an abridged version of the story collection originally published as *The Adventures of Spider: West African Folktales*.

Little, Brown and Company

Hachette Book Group

237 Park Avenue, New York, NY 10017

Visit our website at www.lb-kids.com

Little, Brown and Company is a division of Hachette Book Group, Inc.

The Little, Brown name and logo are trademarks of Hachette Book Group, Inc.

The publisher is not responsible for websites (or their content) that are not owned by the publisher.

First Abridged Edition: May 2012

Originally published in *The Adventures of Spider: West African Folktales* in January 1964 by Little, Brown and Company

ISBN 978-0-316-20381-4

10 9 8 7 6 5 4 3 2 1

SC

Printed in China

Contents

Introduction

IN WEST AFRICA people love to listen to stories. Sometimes at night, when the moon is high, everyone in the village comes out into the wide, clean place where people sit and talk.

Everyone sits in a circle. "Let us call the storyteller," someone cries.

"Tell us a story about Spider," cry the children.

Everyone knows about Spider. He is a favorite character in the stories of West Africa.

He is clever and mischievous. He loves to eat and he hates to work. He plays so many tricks that he gets into a lot of trouble. But when he is good, he is full of fun.

As the storyteller speaks, he strikes his stick upon the ground. "Once upon a time," he says . . .

How Spider Got a Bald Head

SPIDER LIVED in a house made of banana leaves beside a small river with his wife, Aso, and his two sons.

One morning Spider awoke early. He felt good all over. He wanted to do something to help someone.

Quite suddenly, he remembered his old mother-in-law. Of course! He would help the old lady plant her rice.

It was a great distance to her farm, and when at last he reached it, he was already quite hungry. He found the old lady bent over the earth planting seed.

"Good morning, my mother," said Spider. "I have come to help you plant the rice."

Aso's mother was overjoyed. "When we

have finished," she said, "we shall have lunch. I know you are fond of beans, my son, and so I will cook the very best ones I have."

She took a great cooking pot and filled it with beans and onions and peppers and tomatoes and meat. Then she went to a small kitchen not far from where Spider was working, and put the pot on a fire to cook. With that, she went to another part of the farm to work.

After a time the beans began to send out a wonderful smell that floated right across the field and into Spider's nose.

How Spider tried not to notice it! But somehow, each time Spider dug a hole and planted a seed, he seemed to take a step closer to the pot of beans.

Finally, he ran over to the cooking pot. He snatched his hat off and put some of the beans into it with a long spoon. And then he ate them. Mmmmm! He looked all around. No one was coming. Quickly he ladled more

beans into his hat, higher and higher, until
the hat was almost full of boiling beans.

Now in another part of the land not very
far away, many people were planting rice.
Suddenly, a flock of rice birds flew down and
began to steal away the seeds. The people
shouted and threw stones at them. The big
birds flew straight into Aso's mother's little
kitchen. There stood Spider with his hat full
of beans.

There was no time to hide them and there was no time to run away. So Spider threw his hat onto his head, and, of course, the beans began to burn. Spider started to shake his head. He jumped up and down and ran around in a circle outside.

The people all noticed the way Spider was acting, and asked him what was the matter.

"I'm doing the hat-shaking dance," shouted Spider, and his head moved faster and faster.

"I must go to my father's village, for it is the time of the hat-shaking festival."

"What is that?" asked the people.

"It comes every year," cried Spider. "I must run right away, because my father will expect me."

And Spider ran down the path that led into the forest. But all the people ran after him, because they wanted to know all about the hat-shaking festival.

All the time the beans were getting hotter
and hotter. At last, Spider could stand it
no longer. He snatched off his hat, and
beans, onions, meat, and peppers scattered
everywhere. Everyone roared with laughter,
for Spider's head was as bald as an egg.

Spider was so ashamed that he asked the
grass to open for him so that he might hide,
and the grass took pity on him and hid him.
That is why Spider still likes to walk
through grass, and, even today, he is
still bald.

How Spider Got a Thin Waist

ONE DAY SPIDER was walking through the forest. It was early morning and he noticed an unusually pleasant smell. It was food! Today was the festival of the harvest. Every village in the big forest was preparing a feast.

Spider's heart jumped for joy. Already he could taste the food on his tongue.

Now, of course, Spider had not done any of the work to deserve such a feast, for Spider did not like to work at all. All day he played in the sun or slept, and he could eat very well by simply visiting all his friends. In fact, he ate more than they did.

Spider knew there were two villages not far from him, and today each village would have a great feast. The two villages were exactly the same distance away from him. But since there were two dinners, he did not know which one he wanted to go to.

At last he had an idea! He could go to them both! He called his elder son, Kuma. Spider took a long rope and tied one end around his waist. The other end he gave to his son.

"Take this rope to the village on the East," he said to Kuma. "When the food is ready, give the rope a hard pull, and I will know it is time for me to come and eat."

Then Spider called his younger son, Kwaku.
Spider took another long rope and tied it
around his waist, just below the first one.

"Kwaku, take this rope to the village on
the West," he said, "and when the food is all
cooked, pull very hard on it. Then I will come
and have my fill."

But unfortunately for Spider, the people
in the East village and in the West village
had their dinners at exactly the same time.
So, of course, Kuma and Kwaku pulled on
both of the ropes at the same time. Poor,
greedy Spider was caught in the middle.

Kuma and Kwaku could not understand

why their father did not come, and they pulled harder all the time. They finally came to look for their father. When they found him, he looked very different. His waistline was thinner than a needle!

Spider never grew fat again. He stayed the same until today. He has a big head and a big body, and a tiny little waist in between.

Why Spider Lives in Ceilings

ONCE UPON A TIME the rainy season came to the forest, as it must come every year. But this time there was more rain than ever before. Nobody had ever seen anything like it. In the morning it beat against the branches of the trees and tore their leaves from them. The small rivers became deep and wide, and covered the sides of their banks.

The animals in the forest were frightened by all the water. And Spider, who had been too lazy to plant his farm or to set his fish traps, had nothing to eat. Worst of all, the great Leopard, who hunts at night, was hungry and had to stalk the forest during the day.

After many days the rain stopped, and Spider set out at once to look for something to eat. He went down the wide path that led to the river. Leopard was also hunting along

the path that led to the river, and Spider and Leopard walked right into each other.

Now usually, Leopard loves a fat and juicy supper. But today he thought even Spider would taste good, and so he tried to look friendly.

"Good afternoon, Mr. Spider," said Leopard. "How do you fare in all this wet weather?"

Now Spider was lazy and very naughty,
but he was not stupid.

"I am well, Mr. Leopard, but I am in a
great hurry," he answered. And with that,
Spider jumped behind a great palm leaf,
and Leopard could not find him. Leopard
roared a roar that echoed against the hills.

"Never mind," he thought after a few
minutes. "I will go to Spider's house. I will
hide behind his door and wait for him to come
back."

Leopard went up the path from the
river. He went into Spider's little house,

put his nose on his great paws, and sat down to wait.

But Spider had guessed exactly what Leopard would do. And as Spider walked along the path to his house, humming to himself, he suddenly cried out:

"Ho! My banana-leaf house!"

Nobody answered. Everything was silent.

"That's funny," said Spider loudly. "My little house always answers me when I call her. I wonder what is wrong."

Once again, with all his might, he shouted, "Ho! My banana-leaf house. How are you?"

And from deep inside the house came a small, high voice. "I am fine, Mr. Spider. Come on in."

Spider burst out laughing. "Now I know where you are, Mr. Leopard, and you shall never catch me," he said.

And with that, he ran as quick as a flash through the window and up to the highest corner of the ceiling. And he is living there still.